**DO NOT REMOVE
CARDS FROM POCKET**

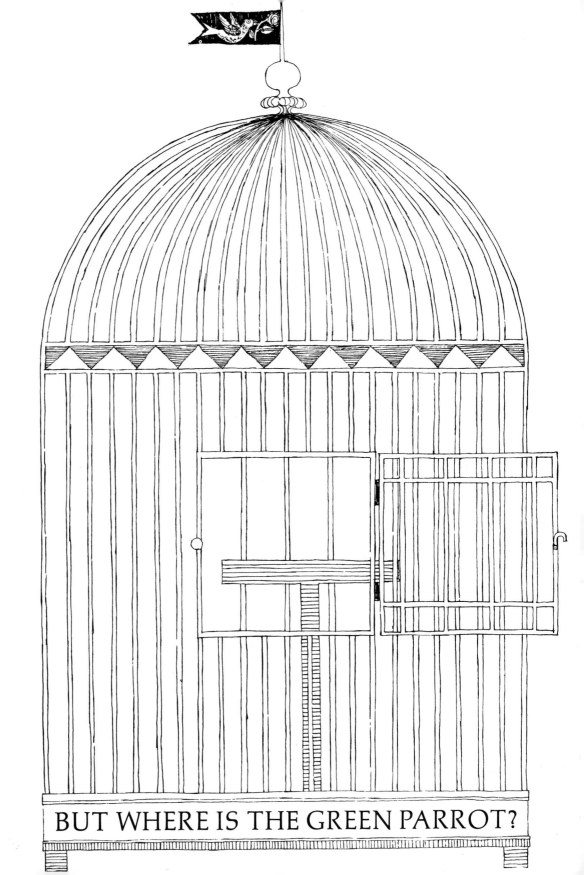

BUT WHERE IS THE GREEN PARROT?

Published by
Delacorte Press / Seymour Lawrence
Bantam Doubleday Dell Publishing Group, Inc.
666 Fifth Avenue
New York, New York 10103

Originally published in German under the title
UND WO IST DE GRÜNE PAPAGEI?

© Sigbert Mohn Verlag, Gütersloh 1965
English translation copyright © 1968 Sigbert Mohn Verlag, Gütersloh

Library of Congress Cataloging in Publication Data

Zacharias, Thomas.
    [Und wo ist der grüne Papagei?]
    But where is the green parrot? : a picture book / by Thomas and
Wanda Zacharias—3rd American ed.
        p. cm.
    Translation of: Und wo ist der grüne Papagei?
    Summary: The brightly colored toys, train, house, or boat are easy
to see, but where is the green parrot? He is in every picture someplace.
    ISBN 0-385-30091-3.—ISBN 0-385-30111-1 (lib. bdg.)
    [1. Parrots—Fiction.   2. Color—Fiction.]   I. Zacharias, Wanda.
II. Title.
PZ7.Z17B   1990
[E]—dc20   89-23761 CIP
                                                          AC
Printed in Italy

June 1990

10 9 8 7 6 5 4 3 2 1

NIL

But Where Is the Green Parrot?

BUT WHERE IS THE GREEN PARROT?

A PICTURE BOOK BY

THOMAS AND WANDA ZACHARIAS

DELACORTE PRESS /
SEYMOUR LAWRENCE

THE TRAIN
has a black engine
with red wheels,
an engine-driver
with a blue coat and cap,

a yellow coach with many windows—

BUT WHERE IS THE GREEN PARROT?

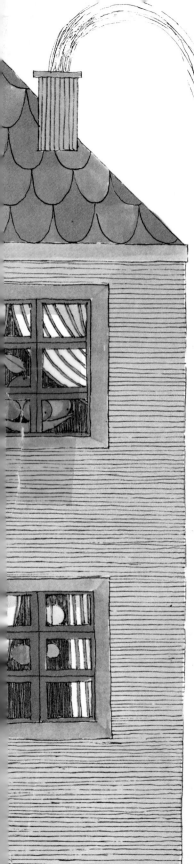

THE HOUSE
has a red roof
with a chimney,
a blue door
with a latch,
a yellow balcony
with flowerpots—
BUT WHERE IS THE GREEN PARROT?

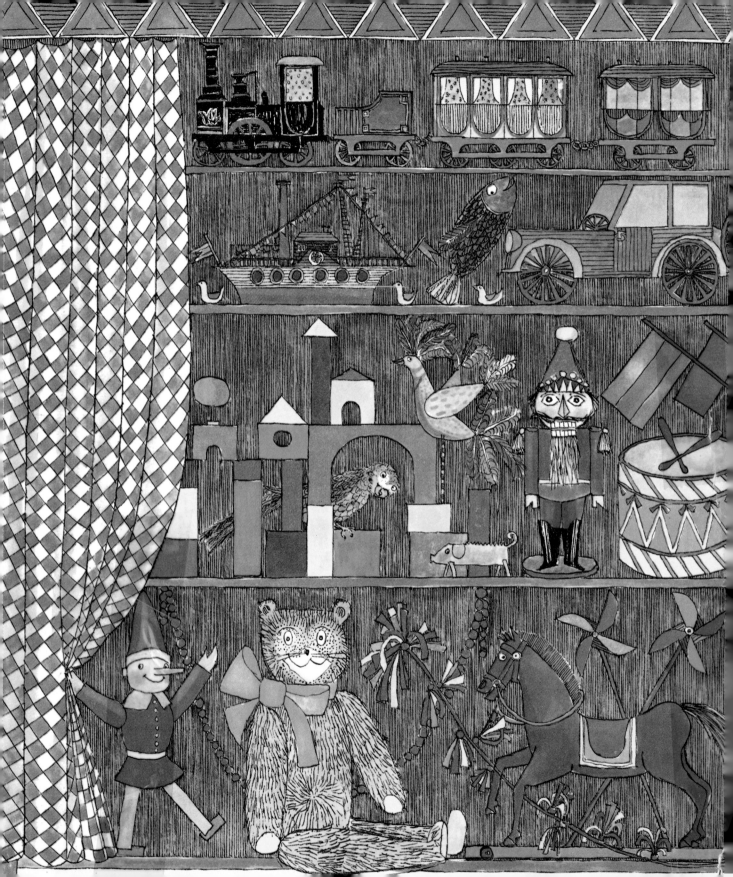

THE TOY CHEST
has a red ball
to throw,
bright wooden blocks
to build with,
a yellow teddy bear
to love—
BUT WHERE IS THE GREEN PARROT?

THE TABLE

has a pink tablecloth
with flowers,
chocolate cake
on a yellow plate,
milk in a blue
mug—

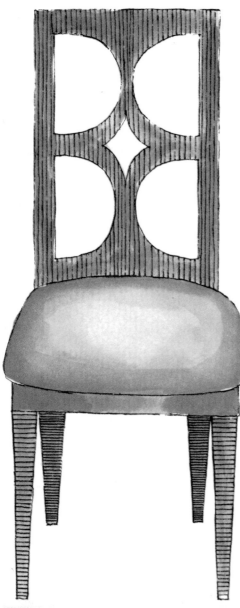

BUT WHERE IS THE GREEN PARROT?

THE GARDEN
has a big tree
heavy with red apples,
a boat
sailing in a birdbath,
a watering can
for the yellow flowers—
BUT WHERE IS THE GREEN PARROT?

THE HORSE
has a red mane
with tight curls,
a blue bridle
with yellow tassels,
a rider in the saddle
with high boots—
BUT WHERE IS THE GREEN PARROT?

THE SHIP
has a red funnel
with black smoke,
a tall mast
with gay flags,
round portholes—
who is looking out?
AND WHERE
IS THE GREEN PARROT?

THE SKY
has the sun
which sometimes shines,
black clouds
which sometimes rain,
flocks of birds
which always fly—
BUT WHERE IS THE GREEN PARROT FLYING?

Do you know where?

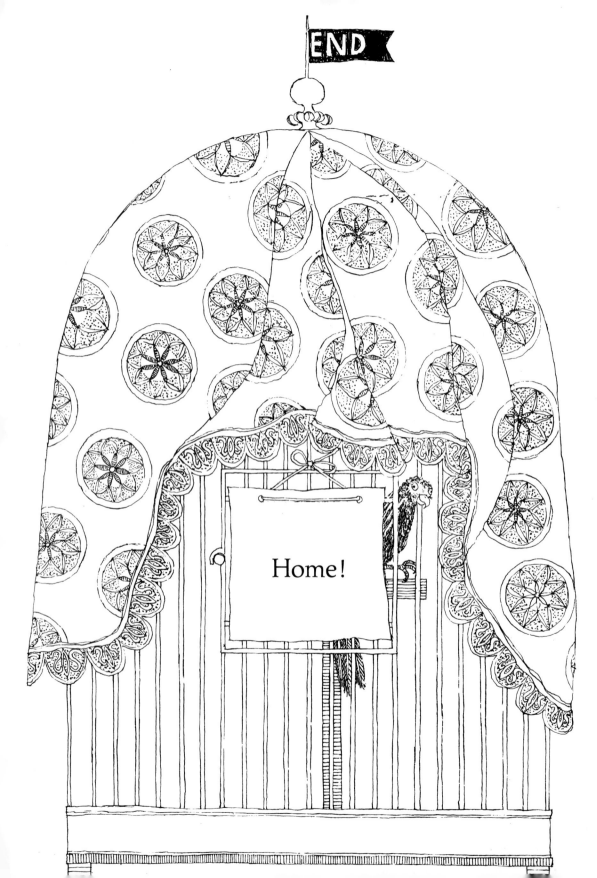

Thomas and Wanda Zacharias have collaborated successfully on a number of children's books. He writes the story and she does the illustrations. They have worked in children's television and were runners-up for the Hans Christian Andersen medal in 1964.